SUGAR WHITE SNOW AND EVERGREENS

A WINTER WONDERLAND OF COLOR

Felicia Sanzari Chernesky

Illustrated by **Susan Swan**

ALBERT WHITMAN & COMPANY
CHICAGO, ILLINOIS

For Dad—and the snows of yesteryear—FSC

For Terry—SS

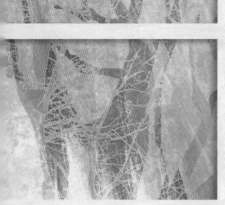

The morning sky was steely **gray**,
and hungry as two bears
we sniffed downstairs but couldn't find
our breakfast anywhere.

Mom said, "Get dressed, my little cubs.
Pull on your **brown** snowsuits.
Grab your scarves and hats and gloves.
Zip up those new snow boots."

"We're going to the farm," Dad said.
"You want to know the reason?
To hunt for winter's hidden gold—
It's maple syrup season!"

Some neighbors and school friends were there.
We had a snowball fight,
then rode a sleigh that made **blue** tracks
through fields of glittering white.

A snowman pointed out the way,
and what do you suppose?
A plump **red** cardinal landed on
his **orange** carrot nose!

We passed a **yellow** tractor chuffing
puffs into the freeze

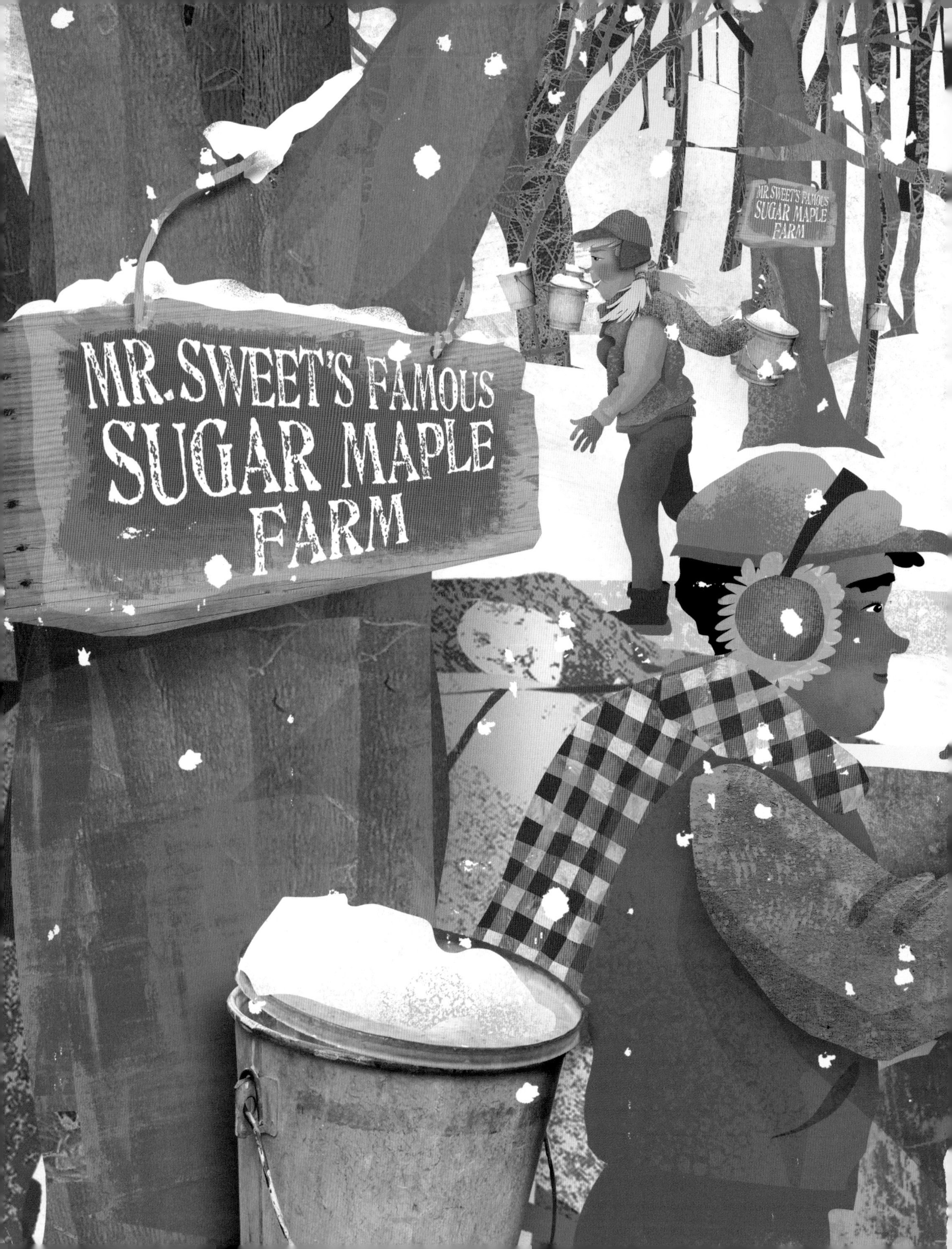

and stopped with bright **pink** cheeks aglow beside some maple trees.

Each tree contained a wooden tap.
A **silver** pail below
collected all the clear, sweet sap.
The farmer said, "Let's go!"

"I'll show you where we boil the sap.
It's called the 'sugar shack.'"
A long and sturdy pan inside
stood bubbling, broad, and **black**.

The **amber** syrup smelled so good
it made our tummies growl.
We hadn't had our breakfast yet
and went out on the prowl.

We rode down hills of **purple** shadows

through rows of **evergreen**.
The farmhouse was the sweetest sight
that we had ever seen!

And while a winter **rainbow** bloomed
on farmhouse coatrack pegs,
we warmed ourselves on pancake smiles
with syrup, hash, and eggs.

Our tummies full, we bundled up
to brave the cold, crisp air
and traveled on—white sun on snow,
bright colors everywhere!

Also by Felicia Sanzari Chernesky and Susan Swan:

Cheers for a Dozen Ears:
A Summer Crop of Counting

Pick a Circle, Gather Squares:
A Fall Harvest of Shapes

Library of Congress Cataloging-in-Publication Data is on file with the publisher.

Text copyright © 2014 by Felicia Sanzari Chernesky
Illustrations copyright © 2014 by Susan Swan
Published in 2014 by Albert Whitman & Company
ISBN 978-0-8075-7234-4
Printed in China
10 9 8 7 6 5 4 3 2 1 BP 18 17 16 15 14

The design is by Nick Tiemersma.

For more information about Albert Whitman & Company,
visit our web site at www.albertwhitman.com.